FOR RAELYN ...
SANTA IS ALWAYS WATCHING.

T'was the night before Christmas
when all through the house...

Wait a minute!

A creature was in fact stirring.

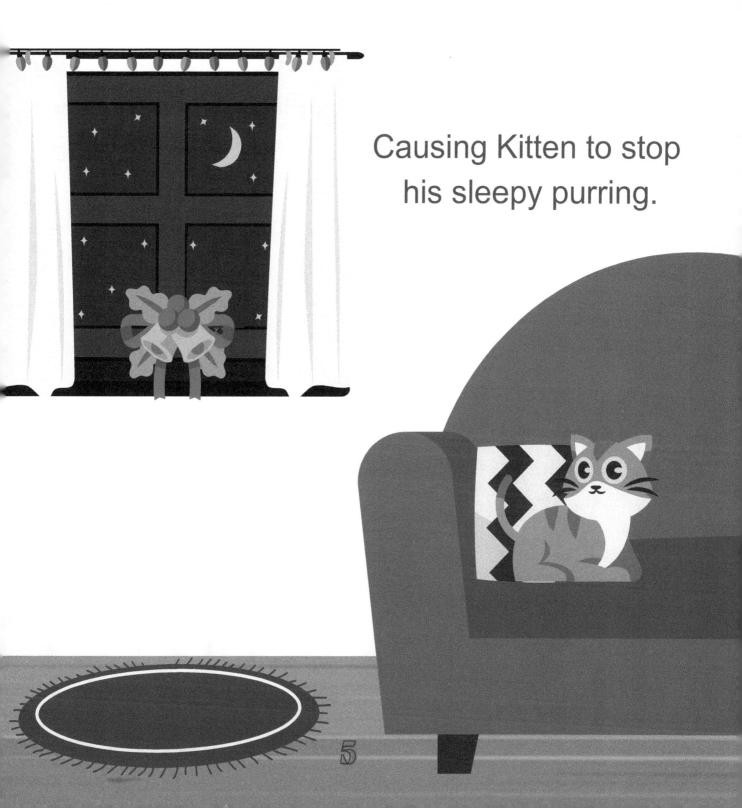

Causing Kitten to stop his sleepy purring.

5

Curiously, a red gift tipped over on one side.

And out walked a present thief with
nothing to hide.

With a quick leap, Kitten extended his
furry paws...

When kitten got ahold of the mouse, he never once thought of dear Santa Claus.

11

When the big man cleared his throat, the fight settled down.

The two stared up at Santa's deep,
disappointed frown.

13

He explained to them that this holiday wasn't just about gifts and present making.

14

It was then that Kitten realized ...

15

That Christmas was about giving, not taking.

16

ABOUT THE AUTHOR

Ashley Clark is an award winning author. With an unending love for fiction and the fantastical, she's always been a mom by day and a writer by night.

She lives in a small town in Illinois with her beautiful daughter, chaotic puppy, and wonderful partner

Printed in the USA
CPSIA information can be obtained
at www.ICGtesting.com
CBHW081120201124
17719CB00006B/21